THE BARKS & BEANS CAFE
MYSTERY SERIES

HOUSE BLEND

THE BARKS & BEANS CAFE MYSTERY SERIES: A
STANDALONE MYSTERY

HEATHER DAY GILBERT

Welcome to the Barks & Beans Cafe, a quaint place where folks pet shelter dogs while enjoying a cup of java...and where murder sometimes pays a visit.

Renovations are underway on the house across the street from the Barks & Beans Cafe, but they come to a screeching halt when the decades-old bones of a missing local woman are unearthed in the basement. When house-flipper Harper shares her concern that no one will buy the place if a murder happened in it, Macy volunteers to help her new friend and do some cold case sleuthing.

As she questions those who knew the victim, Macy turns up a fresh lead. But when she makes the mistake of knocking down a retaining wall of lies, she places herself in the demolition zone with a desperate killer.

Join siblings Macy and Bo Hatfield as they sniff out crimes in their hometown...with plenty of dogs along for the ride! The Barks & Beans Cafe cozy mystery series features a small town, an amateur sleuth, and no swearing or graphic scenes. Find all the books at heatherdaygilbert.com!

The Barks & Beans Cafe series in order:
    Book 1: No Filter
    Book 2: Iced Over
    Book 3: Fair Trade

1

I GLANCED over at the striking woman sitting alone at a small table in our cafe. She'd come in every morning for the past two and a half weeks, getting a caramel cold brew and whatever pastry our baker, Charity, had put on display that morning. She had a longer, narrow nose and impressive cheekbones, but the most noticeable thing about her was the pure white streak that ran through her long bangs and spilled into her mane of cocoa-colored hair. It was impossible to guess if she was in her late thirties, like me, or a decade older. There was some kind of ageless quality about her.

On her fourth visit, when one of our aggressively friendly regulars had commented that she was too young to have white hair, she'd leveled a smile on the woman and said, "You haven't walked a mile in my boots, though, honey."

I knew from that moment we would be friends.

I'd gone straight over to introduce myself as Macy

Hatfield, a co-owner of the cafe. I'd explained that the other co-owner was my brother, Bo, the redhead who was often behind the counter. I told her that Bo was in charge of the Beans section, since he'd come out of the coffee industry, and I ran the Barks section, where shelter dogs got to frolic to their hearts' content and meet potential adoptive customers.

She said she'd really enjoyed drinking her coffee each morning while watching the dogs play. Her name was Harper Pine, and she was the one flipping the house across the street from the cafe. It was easy to relax in our cafe while keeping an eye out the window on her work crew.

But today, Harper's eyes didn't travel to the Barks section once. Instead, she kept glancing at her phone and staring anxiously out the window. She'd barely touched her chocolate croissant.

I looked down at Lola, the black-and-white shelter dog who'd settled onto my lap. She had the most adorable black paw print marking on her back, and she seemed to want nothing more than to be close to me. But something was clearly bothering Harper, so I gently placed Lola on the floor and lured her into the toy area with a treat. After washing my hands, I headed through the gate into the cafe section.

I walked directly to Harper's table and asked, "Is everything okay?"

She shook her head. "To be honest, we've been off schedule for two weeks now. Something came up that's slowed our progress...and now it's going to be all over the news, so I'm concerned that my crews won't be able to catch up."

"The news? That sounds serious." I sat down next to her.

Her olive-green eyes met mine and she lowered her voice. "Early into our renovation, we found a body that had been buried in the basement. Actually, it was just bones, to be precise. The police had to bag them and send them off to a forensic anthropologist at a university to find out who it was. But they've gotten the report back, so now we know."

I didn't want to seem nosy and ask for a name, but Harper seemed to want to explain.

She said, "You're from the area, right? Would you have known a Delta Buckner? She went missing back in the late Eighties, from what I understand."

I shook my head. "I would've been pretty little then."

She took a sip of coffee. "Oh, of course. I just assumed you might've heard her mentioned. The police detective told me it caused a big stir at the time, although he had only just entered the force."

"You've spoken with Detective Hatcher, then?" Charlie Hatcher was our local police detective, and Bo and I considered him a friend—largely because Bo was a retired DEA officer, and Charlie liked to tap him for help with certain cases.

"Yes. He's been so helpful with all of this. I can get a little...let's say *determined*...about staying on target when I flip houses, and this bone discovery definitely threw me for a loop, but the detective has stayed on top of the situation, making sure forensics moved along as quickly as possible. I've been impressed."

I nodded. "Charlie's great. But why would Delta have been buried in a basement?"

A shaft of sunlight lit Harper's white streak, giving the impression she was wearing a halo. "I'm sure it's okay to tell you, since the whole sordid scoop will be on the news tonight, but she had a fractured skull bone, so she must've been hit with a heavy object before she died. It's an official homicide investigation now. That's why I'm concerned we're going to get even further behind schedule."

Something caught my eye near the gate to the Barks section. I turned that way, only to see Lola's wet dog snout, shoved between the bars. She was actively sniffing at the food in the cafe.

With a sudden, hungry whine, she yanked her nose out and leapt straight into the air. Usually my shelter-owner friend Summer warned me of dogs that might have issues when she dropped them off, but she'd likely been unaware of Lola's soft spot for human food.

"I'd better get back to the dogs," I said. "But maybe I could get more details from you later. As a Lewisburg native, I might be able to talk to the people who knew Delta —they could have some information that would move the investigation along."

Harper clasped her hands together. "That would be wonderful. I have a feeling that even if this is the most gorgeous flip ever, no one will buy it if they think Delta was killed there and her murderer is still on the loose. I'm anxious to wrap this thing up. My crew's been antsy ever since they dug up the bones."

I nodded. "It's a gruesome thing." I glanced over at Bo, who was standing at the coffee bar, pouring milk into a coffee drink. I had a sudden brainstorm. "Say, would you like to come to my brother's house tonight and join us for dinner? We're planning to grill on the deck for the first time this spring. He always makes plenty of food, and I'm positive he wouldn't mind. Then we could talk more."

She looked surprised to be asked, and I got the fleeting impression she didn't get out much beyond her trips to our cafe. "Oh, sure, I'd love to come. Could I bring something?"

"Just yourself." As Lola gave another leap, I said, "Give me your number and I'll text you the directions."

As I'd guessed, Bo okayed the plan to have Harper over. His sky-blue eyes twinkled as he said, "I bought plenty of chicken, and I'm anxious to try out a new barbeque recipe I got. You want to bring chips?"

My big brother knew I wasn't the best cook. Left to my own devices, I often wound up eating frozen pizza or sub sandwiches for supper. "Sure. I'll make some French onion dip, too."

"Thanks, sis." His short-cut hair, as well the tattoos on his upper arms, spoke of his time as a Marine. Although he now sported a beard, he kept it trimmed at all times. In short, my brother was the kind of guy who attracted lots of attention from customers, but he was a one-woman man, and his woman was Summer. We always had a good time hanging out together, and I was glad she'd be over for our meal tonight, too.

Bo shot me a serious look. "Am I missing my guess, or did you have some kind of ulterior motive in inviting

Harper over? You two looked like you were having an intense conversation."

I nodded. As usual, my brother saw right through me. I explained what Harper had told me about the discovery of Delta's bones in the basement.

"I wondered why things seemed to have slowed down across the street," Bo said. "I'm glad they figured out whose body it was—I vaguely recall rumors flying at the time about what had become of Delta. I think most people assumed she'd left her husband. Maybe now the construction crew can get to work in earnest. I can't wait to see the finished product, which will only up the curb appeal on this street. Harper seems to be quickly building a reputation as the meticulous kind of house-flipper you'd want to renovate an older home."

"You'll have to talk with her about the cafe," I said. "The first time I met her, she mentioned that she loved the way you'd redesigned this house."

The Barks & Beans Cafe occupied the front half of the large Colonial home Bo and I had grown up in with our great-aunt Athaleen, who'd adopted us when our parents had died in a sudden creek flood. Now I lived in the back half with my rescued Great Dane, Coal, and Bo had his own bungalow a couple of houses up the street. The cafe had been his brainchild. He wanted to offer me a career doing what I loved in my beloved home state of West Virginia after my ex-husband walked out on me.

Bo joked, "Have you paired Harper up with one of the shelter dogs yet?"

I'd recently told him I was starting to feel like a doggie/human matchmaker, since I was always looking for ways to place shelter dogs with just the right customers. But there was no shame in giving people nudges toward a mutually enriching relationship with a lonely shelter dog.

"You know, I haven't even asked her if she has a dog yet." I'd remedy that oversight tonight.

2

AFTER WORK, I headed up the sidewalk to my half of the house, taking time to sniff the lilac bushes that were loaded with blooms this year. May was my favorite month, and not only because my birthday fell in it. After a long, cold winter, it felt like the mountains gave a collective gasp, then reluctantly allowed the persistent sunlight to warm them. Delicate swaths of fog blanketed the greened-up hills in the mornings, and a bullfrog chorus filled the ponds at night. I was able to open my windows, so for a few weeks, my home maintained the perfect temperature with no heating or air conditioning costs.

I'd turned 39 only a few days ago, and we'd had a small party at the cafe. My boyfriend, Titan, had called from Virginia, since he was working a job and couldn't come in to visit. He'd sent me a beautiful bouquet of fuchsia-colored roses, as well as a hanging plant for my porch. The last year in my thirties was off to a wonderful start.

As usual, Coal was standing directly behind my door as I unlocked and opened it. He bounded onto the porch, but made an immediate effort to control his excitement by sitting down next to me. His strong black tail whapped against my leg, the only indication of his frenzied affection. I gave him a thorough head rub, then said, "Go potty," which sent him rushing down the stairs and into the flower garden.

A cheery voice sounded from the sidewalk. "And how was the cafe today?" My neighbor Vera's short white hair came into view, and she halted next to my back gate.

Coal gave a huge bellow since he'd been taken off-guard, but I immediately shushed him. It was hardly unusual for Vera to walk her golden Labradoodle, Waffles, past our place. But Coal and Waffles were sworn frenemies, determined to bark at each other from their respective sides of the fence, even though, deep down, they kind of liked each other.

I jogged over to say hello. "Work went fine, but I did have something I wanted to ask you about. Years ago, did you by any chance know a lady named Delta Buckner?"

Vera's brown eyes widened and she fluttered a hand to her chest. "Why, yes—I surely knew her. She went missing after a baby shower I attended, and she hasn't been heard from since. Why were you asking?"

Knowing it would be all over the news soon, I figured it wouldn't hurt to give Vera a heads-up. "They found her body—her bones—buried in the basement at that house they're renovating across from the cafe. It looks like someone hit her in the head before she died."

Vera gasped and leaned against my fence. Waffles gave a prolonged whine and sat down, as if sensing something was off with her owner.

"Lawsie," Vera said. "Murdered! And she was in the

basement, you say? But that wasn't even her house...she lived a couple of houses down. I can't even believe it. I haven't heard Delta mentioned for years." She took a deep breath and gazed into the distance. "Well, the baby shower was for Chrissy Evans—she went to our church. Let me think...there were several of us at Chrissy's house that day. Your great-aunt Athaleen was there, of course, as well as the pastor's wife, Judy. She's living in Wyoming now. Then there was Diana Minor, who's since passed. Suzanne Payette was there, too. Oh, and Chrissy's mother Linnie Hancock was there to write down who gave what, and Matilda Crump was also living here at that time, so she was there." Vera gave a sigh. "She's always been the type to show up at showers, even when she's hardly close to the expecting mother."

Matilda Crump was a widow and a true piece of work—she spoke whatever she was thinking, no matter how rude it might come off. At some point, she'd adopted an affected British accent, even though she'd only visited England once.

"Do you remember anything specific about the shower?" I asked.

Vera looked thoughtful. "Chrissy didn't want to find out the gender—I recall that. It was the early days of ultrasounds, you see. She got a lot of yellow and green things. I believe I went in on a baby swing with the pastor's wife. They served Swedish meatballs, and Athaleen and I brought a vegetable tray. Linnie had some kind of green punch concoction that wasn't very tasty."

This wasn't quite the type of insider information I'd been looking for, but maybe Vera would circle around to a more helpful memory.

"Chrissy and Delta were best friends—they'd grown up near each other," Vera added. "But they couldn't have looked more different. Chrissy had a blonde perm, and Delta had the straightest black hair you ever saw."

"What about Delta's marriage?" I asked. "Did she have any children?"

"She claimed things were great, but Delta always was one of those women with a 'roving eye.' She tended to flirt with any men in the vicinity. She went missing before she had children."

"What happened to her husband?"

"William Sylvester—nicknamed 'Billy'—moved away several years later. He's just over in Raleigh County, though, so he didn't go far." Vera held up a finger. "Say, I have a good idea. You could go over and talk to the detective who headed up the investigation. It was Mercer Priestly—I've mentioned him to you before. He's a kind man, and he was close with your great-aunt after Clive died. In fact, they dated a little while. She dropped him for some reason she never told me, but they stayed friends after. I'm sure he wouldn't mind speaking to you, especially if you explained who you are. I'll text you his number."

Waffles suddenly jumped to her feet to sniff at a passing butterfly. Coal, who was keeping a sharp eye over the fence, gave a deep bark. I dropped my hand to his head. "Quiet."

As Waffles tugged on her leash, Vera gave a reluctant shake of her head. "I'm afraid I can't remember anything important about that day. I spoke to the police afterward— we all did—but none of us noticed anything strange. Mercer would be your best bet."

Knowing Waffles was ready to get going, I said, "Thanks for your help, Vera. I'll look into it."

Once the curly Doodle had frisked off down the sidewalk, Coal moseyed back to his garden-sniffing venture. Wishing Auntie A had kept a diary so I could get an inside track on why she'd broken up with Mercer, I headed into the house to make the French onion dip.

THE SMELL of grilled chicken wafted toward me as I walked Coal into Bo's house. Stormy, Bo's Calico cat, was positioned on her cat tower perch, but when she saw Coal, she jumped down and gave a prolonged stretch of her back. Apparently, this was cat language for "You may approach her royal highness," since Coal promptly crept forward, then dropped onto the floor directly in front of her. Stormy, who had every bit as much spirit as her name would indicate, gave Coal an affectionate pat on the nose, then made a swift leap back to her tower platform. The dynamics between my hundred and sixty-five-pound Dane and the eleven-pound Calico never ceased to amuse me.

I glanced around, noticing Bo had bought a new wicker swing and fastened it into the ceiling. It was no accident that his bungalow felt exactly like a beach house. My brother liked vacationing by the sand and surf, while I preferred heading even deeper into the mountains.

After carrying the chips and dip onto the back patio, I found that Harper had already arrived and was deep in conversation with Bo. From what I could gather, they were discussing the assassination attempt on Ronald Reagan, which was quite the unusual topic. But something had told me that Harper was far from your usual girl.

She turned and gave me a hug. "Thanks so much for asking me over tonight. I can't wait to sink my teeth into that barbeque. It smells tantalizing."

"My brother's a pro." Turning to Bo, I asked, "Summer's not here yet?"

"She had a last-minute adoption, she said. I think it was that paw print dog you had in the Barks section today—was her name Lola?"

"Oh, that's great! She was such a sweetie."

As Bo took chicken from the grill and placed it on a platter, I turned back to Harper. "I asked my neighbor Vera about Delta. As it turns out, she was at the baby shower the day Delta went missing."

Harper was all ears. She sat down in Bo's turquoise rocking chair and I took a seat nearby. "Did she have any thoughts on what had happened?"

"She was appalled to find out Delta had been murdered. Said she'd been a bit of a flirt, but her marriage seemed okay. She recommended I speak with the detective at that time, Mercer Priestly."

Bo abruptly looked up from his grilling. "Mercer, you said?"

"Yeah—why? Do you know him?" I asked.

"He's a good guy." Bo's voice was unusually gruff, the way it sounded when he was getting emotional.

Hoping Harper hadn't noticed Bo's out-of-character reaction, I said, "I'm going to text him soon. Have the police told you anything new?"

Harper rocked her chair at a brisk pace, as if she had

energy to burn. "Just that they've contacted Delta's husband Billy. Detective Hatcher said Billy actually sounded relieved when he heard. I guess he'd always believed she'd run away from their marriage. Oh—and the detective also told me the story has been released to the news."

Summer stepped onto the patio, smiling at us before walking over and giving Bo a kiss on the cheek. "Doggie adoption successful," she announced. "Miss Lola has a great new home. One of your cafe customers bonded with her this afternoon." She walked our way and extended a hand toward Harper. "Hi. I'm Summer Adkins."

Harper smiled. "And I'm Harper Pine."

"Nice to meet you. Any friend of the Hatfield siblings is a friend of mine," Summer said. "Now, what were you saying was on the news? I only caught the tail end of your conversation."

I caught Summer up on the discovery of Delta's bones in the place Harper was flipping.

"That house has been standing empty for a little while. Who would've guessed there were bones moldering in the basement?" Summer shivered.

Harper said, "It had only been up for sale about a year when I got it. Beverly Dunford was the owner—she was looking to unload the place after her mother died. Her mom was Irma Jean Lilly, and she was the one who bought the place in 1991—a couple of years after Delta went missing. Of course, Beverly was horrified to discover her mom had been living in a house with bones in the basement."

"So the place was vacant from 1989 to 1991?" I asked.

"According to the documentation we found when I

bought it, yes," Harper said. "It took awhile to sell to Irma Jean."

Coal's massive face appeared in the glass doorway. "Would you mind if I let my dog come out on the porch?" I asked Harper. "He's huge, but he won't bite."

Harper's face brightened. "Go right ahead. Big dogs don't scare me."

I opened the door and Coal plodded out. He gave a polite glance toward Harper, then sat down in front of me.

"He's very well-mannered," Harper said.

I was glad to see she didn't try to pet Coal, which might've made him nervous. Instead, she sat still. Finally, Coal stood and moved Harper's way, sniffing at her hand on the armrest. She slowly petted behind his glossy ears, and Coal looked at her like she was his new best friend.

"He likes you," I observed.

Harper kept her eyes on Coal, but I could tell they had welled up with unshed tears. "I had a German Shepherd for eleven years. When she died, I couldn't handle being around dogs. But since I've been visiting the cafe, I feel like I'm easing back into things. Maybe someday I'll find one again."

Obviously, Harper had formed a deep friendship with her German Shepherd, the way I had with Coal. I couldn't imagine how devastated I'd be if something happened to him.

Bo set the chicken on the table. "Time to eat," he announced.

Coal stood and walked to the far edge of the patio and sat down. He knew he wasn't allowed to come near the food.

As we filled our plates, I asked if Harper was enjoying her stay in Lewisburg, despite the setbacks to her house flip.

"I'm renting the bottom floor of an older house in town," she said. "It's comfortable enough, but I wish I could flip that place, too."

"Would the owner consider selling?" Summer spooned a pile of pasta salad onto her plate.

Harper shook her head. "I run all my decisions through my investor, and I don't think he'd want that one. There aren't many period details left in it. Speaking of which—Bo, you did a great job renovating the cafe."

Bo launched into the ins and outs of what he'd done to Auntie A's house. We all helped ourselves to plenty of chicken, which had turned out perfectly crispy on the outside and tender on the inside. As we each had one of the chocolate chip cookies Summer had brought, Coal headed toward the door. He was obviously anxious to get back to Stormy before we had to leave, so I let him in.

When Bo and Summer headed inside to clean up, Harper said, "I'd better get on back. We have an early day tomorrow, since we're trying to make up for lost time."

"I had a question," I said. "Since Delta's bones were in the basement, are you going to have to pour new concrete?"

"It wasn't a concrete floor, actually. Just packed dirt with one of those artificial grass carpet remnants laid over it. When my crew shifted an old chest freezer down there, they noticed the dirt beneath it wasn't very well-packed. They poked around a little and turned up a bone. Whoever buried Delta didn't get her that deep, apparently." She raised a dark eyebrow. "Actually, I'm stopping by there on my way back to make sure everything's ready to roll tomorrow. Would you want to go with me and see where they found her?"

I didn't hesitate. "Sure—I'll drop off Coal and then we can walk over."

Interestingly, I was beginning to spot some similarities between Harper with Bo. Neither of them could sit around and relax when there was work to be done. I could tell Harper was single-minded in her determination to get her reno project back on track, and I wanted to help her any way I could.

While it seemed a little macabre to check out a hole where a murdered woman's body had been buried, it might help to see the scene before I talked with Mercer Priestly. He would doubtless be curious as to any details about the discovery of the woman he'd searched for so earnestly back in the Eighties. Vera had texted me his number, so I hoped we could set up a meeting soon.

3

THE HOUSE Harper was flipping was quaint, but it was hard for me to see how it had any potential to be beautiful. The two-story was much smaller than my Colonial, and its taupe-colored exterior paint had chipped off in numerous places. The roof of the covered porch sagged against the cheap columns.

As we walked up the stairs, Harper said, "This is a Craftsman style house, but you wouldn't believe it to look at the outside. The pillars need to be heavier to be true to the era and the paint job was hideous, but we're going to fix all that." She stuck the key in the lock. "Wait'll you see the inside, though."

Once she'd switched on the antique pendant light, I immediately understood what she was talking about. We walked through a wide wooden archway into the living room, which featured half a wall of windows surrounded by original-looking wooden trim. Built-in bookshelves framed a brick-lined fireplace on the far side of the room.

"This is amazing," I said.

"Right? Once I saw the interior in the online realty photos, I knew we had to flip it. I could visualize the look I wanted the woodwork to have—matte, not glossy. I mean, look at the rich grain of it!" Her eyes met mine. "Sorry—I'm getting all nerdy on you. Let's head to the basement."

"No rush. I'm enjoying soaking it all in. I know you have quite a ways to go to finish this place, but it really is the type of house that should get snatched up in this town. It's like the definition of cozy." I glanced at the bookshelves again. "I could see myself sitting there in a worn velvet armchair, reading on a rainy day."

She nodded. "Artsy. That's how I think of it. A haven for an artist." Leading me through the dining room, she said, "The basement is right off the kitchen."

The interior wall of the kitchen had been torn down to the studs, and it looked like the crew was working on expanding the space. Harper led the way to a white wooden doorway tucked into the corner.

Flipping on the light at the top of the stairs, she explained, "The basement hasn't been used in years, so we have quite a few outdated appliances to haul out. I think the washing machine dates back to the Seventies. When Mrs. Lilly moved in, she turned a closet into an upstairs laundry room and abandoned the one in the basement, since she had trouble going up and down stairs. She also changed a downstairs guest room into her master suite." She headed down the stairs.

Brushing a cobweb away as I ducked beneath a low beam, I asked, "What was your crew doing in the basement again?"

"Checking out the plumbing and heating systems, but

they were also trying to determine if we needed to pour a concrete floor to keep the moisture down. It turns out, we are going to have to do concrete—once the police give us the all-clear, that is." She sighed.

"This is quite a process." We'd reached the basement's dirt floor, where the green carpet had been rolled to one side. A rusted-out chest freezer had been pushed against the wall, and I could see the gaping hole in the floor next to it.

A sudden wave of apprehension rolled over me, and I stopped short. Harper turned around. "You okay? There's nothing in there now."

"I know. It just hit me that someone shoved Delta's lifeless body into the dirt, like a sack of potatoes."

"Actually, it wasn't quite that slipshod." Harper flipped on her phone flashlight and shone it on the hole, which appeared quite shallow. "Even though the person must've been in a hurry because they didn't dig the hole very deep, Delta's body had been wrapped in a shower curtain, so she wasn't just dropped in there. Forensics checked out the curtain, and even though it's deteriorated some, they could tell it was one of those dime-a-dozen plastic shower curtains everyone had back then. Unfortunately, there's no way to trace it."

I stepped closer, sending a dirt clod rattling to the bottom of the hastily dug hollow. "I can't understand how the killer got in, since the house was on the market and would've been locked up. Was a break-in reported around the time Delta vanished? It seems like that would've raised red flags."

Harper shook her head. "Detective Hatcher said there

were no reports of anything suspicious in this neighborhood."

"Maybe the person already had the key...like the home owner before Irma Jean bought it. Do you know who that was?"

She looked dubious. "Sure—I did my homework on the place. Before Mrs. Lilly, it was owned by a couple who moved out West...California, I think? But that doesn't make sense on a couple of levels. First of all, they would've had to travel across the country to murder Delta. And even if they had gone to all that effort, why would they have risked drawing attention to themselves by hiding a murdered body in their own basement?"

"You're right. I didn't really think that all the way through." I followed her up the steps. "What about someone at the realty company? They would've had a key."

"It was sold by Robbins Realty. I noted that when doing a title search. Their company is actually still around. It's right down the street from the place I'm renting." Harper dodged an old sink that was lying in the floor as she walked back toward the stairs.

"You have your hands full with renovations, so I'll check into it," I offered. "I'm off tomorrow, so I'll check to see if they're open on Saturdays. In the meantime, I'll text Mercer Priestly and see if he might have time to talk."

Harper flipped off the light and we stepped into the kitchen again. "That would be great. I don't want to put an extra burden on you, but you obviously know what you're doing, and I don't have time to follow up on things right now. Let me know if you need any help from me, though—

I'll drop what I'm doing to clear this black cloud looming over my renovation."

"Sounds good. I actually have some experience in these kinds of things."

She gave me a sharp look. "Looking for murderers, you mean?"

I didn't want to scare away my new friend, so I tried to brush it off. "I've just helped out here and there."

But Harper wasn't so easily deterred. I suddenly got the feeling her green eyes were seeing all the things I wasn't saying. "That's admirable. Don't be ashamed of helping the course of justice." With that enigmatic remark, she led the way toward the front porch, where she locked up the house.

Once she had headed off toward her place, I made my way across the street, pondering our discussion.

While there was a *lot* to Harper Pine that met the eye—namely, her white-streaked mane, her discerning green gaze, and her serious house-flipping know-how—she had far more hidden beneath the surface. Although I'd been initially impressed by her boldness, now I realized we shared a commitment to finding the truth.

In fact, Harper Pine seemed like a force to be reckoned with, and she wasn't about to roll over and let a cold homicide case slow her momentum for long. The least I could do was help her speed the process along.

MERCER PRIESTLY TEXTED BACK about thirty minutes after I contacted him. His text was beautifully old-fashioned, like he was writing a proper letter for English class. Coal curled up by my feet as I read it.

"Dear Miss Hatfield, I would only be too happy to have you drop by, perhaps around one in the afternoon tomorrow, if that is convenient. I rarely have visitors these days, but I do know how to make a good cup of coffee, which I'm happy to offer you. I've been in contact with Charlie Hatcher in regard to the Delta Buckner case, and he has given me free rein to answer any of your pressing questions. I'm not sure how much aid I can provide, but it will be a delight to see you again." He'd shared his address at the end.

Given his terminology, I assumed Mercer must've met me before, probably when I was young. Unfortunately, I didn't have many memories of those years, so I wondered if I'd recognize him.

Before heading up to bed, I rummaged around in my bookshelves. In high school, I'd bought a book of Edgar Allan Poe's short stories, and I felt pretty certain I'd kept it. I wanted to reread one of them.

I managed to locate the well-worn paperback and thumbed through to the story I was looking for: *The Cask of Amontillado.*

In the story, a man seeking revenge takes his enemy to his crypt, giving him wine before placing him in fetters. He then starts building a stone wall to hold him in—while his enemy is fully lucid. It was bone-chilling the first time I'd read it, and now, knowing Delta had been buried—albeit not alive—in a basement, I could hardly bear the heartless description of narrator's deliberate entombing of the one who'd insulted him.

What had Delta's murderer been motivated by? Hatred? Love? Jealousy?

As I read online about Poe's ghoulish tale, I learned he might've written *The Cask of Amontillado* as a retaliation toward an author who'd mocked his writing. While that was a creative way of taking out authorly frustration, it certainly seemed Poe had an unnatural flair for slipping into the homicidal psyche.

Next, I skimmed over *The Tell-Tale Heart*, cringing as its unhinged murderer shared how he had gone about his gruesome crime.

Had Delta encountered a calculating real-life madman, like the ones portrayed in Poe's books? Or had her death been an unplanned crime of passion? A skull fracture was not a gentle way to go.

Coal was obviously ready to go to sleep, having settled onto his large pillow at the foot of my bed. I placed my Poe book on the nightstand and flipped off my lamp. As a light spring rain pattered against my windows, I burrowed into bed, pulling my quilt up over my arms. It was just the right weight for this weather.

But I couldn't get comfortable as I envisioned Delta's body, crammed into that hole. Had the shower curtain been a thoughtful addition in order to protect her body from the dirt? Or had it merely been a practical decision, keeping it from smelling bad and getting discovered?

Decades had passed since Delta's murder. Perhaps it was hopeless for me to look into things at this stage. After all, the police would've investigated thoroughly in 1989. But the final piece of the puzzle had not yet been revealed— Delta's body.

Harper had already invested so much time and effort into her house renovation. It would be a shame if the freshly flipped house sat on the market as it had in the past.

No, it couldn't hurt to look into a few things. Especially on the off-chance I'd come across new information for the police. Delta's friends and her husband—if he wasn't the murderer—deserved to know what had happened to her.

4

AFTER SLEEPING in the next morning, I ate a late lunch before driving to Mercer Priestly's home in nearby Fairlea. It was sprinkling rain as I followed his long driveway up to a ranch-style brick house. I pulled my jacket hood up and jogged up to his front porch, but before I could even ring the bell, the door opened.

"Macy Hatfield, as I live and breathe." Mercer's blue eyes were friendly. "You still have that headful of strawberry blonde hair, I see."

"Yes, and it's still as unmanageable as it ever was—especially in weather like this." I extended my hand to shake his. He had a firm grip, but it wasn't uncomfortably tight. I had the feeling Mercer was the kind of trustworthy person I could confide in, which must've been how Auntie A had felt about him, too.

His eyes held mine, and I sensed we were thinking about the same person. "Your great-aunt...she was a special person in my life," he said haltingly. "It grieved me when she found out about the cancer."

"It came as a shock to all of us, but mercifully, she wasn't in pain for long." I took a deep breath to clear my mind of the memories of Auntie A's final days. "You said we'd met before. I can't recall when that was."

"You were just a little tyke then, playing with your dolls and dogs. Your brother took to me quickly and followed me around every time I visited." He looked thoughtful. "I should have dropped by your cafe sooner to reconnect, but I didn't want to make things awkward for either of you."

"I'm sure Bo would be happy to see you again," I said. "Drop in anytime."

"Maybe I will." He gestured toward the couch nearest the door. "Have a seat, though, and I'll get us something to drink. Would you like hot tea, coffee, or maybe a glass of iced sweet tea?"

"Coffee with milk or cream sounds perfect."

As Mercer walked into the kitchen, I examined the photos on his side table. He didn't appear to have children or grandchildren. I wondered if he'd been a bachelor all these years. His furniture was tasteful, if modest, and rather well-worn.

On the mantel over his fireplace, he had several awards that looked law enforcement related. Clearly, Mercer Priestly had been an impressive police detective in his day.

He brought out a tray with two mugs of coffee and set it on the low table in front of me. "I hope that's enough cream."

I glanced into the mug. "That looks perfect." After taking a sip, I said, "I appreciate your time. I just thought you'd have a unique perspective on what might have happened to Delta Buckner. As you know, Detective

Hatcher is a personal friend, and I'm just doing a little digging into the past to help him out."

Mercer nodded. "I've heard about your exploits, Macy, so there's no need to be humble. You and Bo have aided Charlie more than once with murder cases. I'll freely tell you that your great-aunt assisted me some, and I was always grateful for her inconspicuous ways of getting information. Fire away, and I'll help all I can."

I asked the first question that came to mind. "Could you tell me who last saw Delta on the day she went missing?"

Mercer's smile faded. "It was actually your neighbor, Vera Cox. She spoke to her after the shower, before they both headed home."

I tried to hide my dismay. "Vera didn't mention that to me."

Mercer sat back in his chair, cradling his mug. "To be honest, I don't think it's important. The truth is, someone else saw her afterward—the murderer. Vera had no motivation to kill Delta, nor do I think she'd manage to clobber someone over the head like that. We were never able to verify that Delta arrived home after the shower, since even though the door to her home was unlocked, she and Billy left it unlocked all the time. You know how it is in a small town." He added, "Her purse vanished along with her, which is why many suspected she'd run away from her husband."

"Did you think that was the case?" I asked.

He ran a hand through his thick salt-and-pepper hair. "I can't tell you how many times I've asked myself that through the years, right up until the day they called and said they'd found Delta's bones. Something always told me she hadn't done a runner, though, since the last thing she told Vera was that she might be next in line for a baby shower."

I sucked in a breath. "Was she pregnant when she died?"

He shrugged. "We'll never know. Bones can indicate if a woman's given birth before, but not if she's pregnant. All the forensics people could say for certain was that she hadn't given birth."

I considered what he'd said. "What about her husband, Billy? What did you think of him, if you don't mind my asking? Did he have any reason to kill her?"

"He was an extremely soft-spoken man who didn't get too worked up about things. He was an appraiser, as I recall." He drained his coffee mug, then stared out the window. "As to what I thought of him...well, that kind of shifted over time. At first, he came off as a genuinely distressed husband who was shocked that his wife had disappeared. But as the years went by, every time I pulled him in to discuss a possible lead, he acted different. Cagey, almost. I never could put my finger on anything unusual about him, but I had the gut feeling he was hiding something important from me."

"Any ideas as to what that might have been?"

"I've asked him all kinds of ways, and he's never admitted anything, but, given how friendly Delta was with men, I always wondered if he hadn't discovered she was having an affair."

"You think they had some kind of fight and he hit her over the head?" I took a sip of coffee, but it had already turned cold. Hoping I hadn't inadvertently made a face, I set the mug on the coffee table.

"I do think it's possible. Maybe he's the sort that comes

off as mild-mannered, but can get completely enraged, like the Incredible Hulk."

"But how could he have gotten into the locked house to bury her?" I considered the options, and only one seemed vaguely feasible. "Maybe he'd recently appraised the house and pocketed the key."

He looked thoughtful, but then frowned. "I doubt it. He'd probably have to get the key from the realtor. The house was listed with Robbins Realty at that time." He leaned in. "Oddly enough, Suzanne Payette owns that business—I think Robbins was her maiden name—and she was also at the baby shower on the day Delta went missing. I told Charlie to follow up on that new angle."

Vera had mentioned that Suzanne was at the shower, too. It wouldn't be hard for me to visit the realty agency, maybe under the pretense of looking for more property where we could expand Barks & Beans someday. It *was* an idea Bo and I had discussed, albeit briefly, when our cafe had started taking off financially, but we weren't anywhere near branching out at this point.

I had one final question. "I've heard that Billy still lives in West Virginia. How did he react to the news that Delta's body had been found, do you know?"

"Charlie drove over to Beckley to break the news in person. The minute Billy opened the door, he guessed that Delta had been found dead. He said he'd always had a gut feeling about it."

I twisted my lip. "Gut feelings are easy to have when you're the one who killed the person."

He looked grim. "I don't think they'll find any DNA evidence at this point, but I'm trying not to give up hope that Delta's murderer will come to light." In a cheerier tone, he added, "Would you like some fresh coffee?"

"Thank you, but I'd probably better get on back. I might drop into the realty place on the way home, since it's my day off."

His blue gaze turned shrewd. "I can see you're like your Aunt Athaleen in more ways than one. She was like a dog with a bone when it came to righting injustice. She couldn't stand to see innocent people get hurt."

My eyes suddenly welled with tears. For the first time in a long time, I felt like someone truly understood one of the core desires driving me. Although I didn't like to admit it, I'd experienced some serious emotional damage in my life —from losing my parents at the age of two to discovering my seemingly smitten husband was cheating on me and wanted a divorce. It almost physically *pained* me to know that anyone I cared about was going through hardship because of a situation that could be rectified.

And it had just been revealed that Delta was murdered and buried in a shallow grave. Surely I might be able to dig up some helpful bits of information, if I talked to enough people who'd been around when she had gone missing.

After thanking Mercer for the coffee and his generous help, I headed out to my car, where I checked on Robbins Realty's hours of business. Sure enough, they stayed open until five. I could drop by and see if Suzanne happened to be in, and, if not, I'd just leave my number and let her know I was checking out properties in the area. That should at least get my foot in the door.

5

ROBBINS REALTY WAS SITUATED in a charming two-story house in town. The navy siding looked freshly painted, and its cream-colored trim provided a striking contrast. Cheery begonias filled the window boxes. As I stepped onto the plush Persian rug, a thirty-something man in a well-fitted suit stood up behind a desk in the corner. He looked like the picture of Southern gentility.

"Welcome to Robbins Realty. Is there anything I could help you with today?"

"Actually, I was wondering if Suzanne happened to be in?" I tried to sound like we were close.

He beamed a white smile at me. "She stepped out back for a moment, but she'll be in soon, I'm sure. Is there anything I could help you with in the meantime?"

"Oh, sure. I was looking into commercial property in the neighboring areas...maybe White Sulphur Springs?"

"That's a charming town. I'd be happy to pull up some properties for you." He sat down behind his laptop and started tapping away.

A woman walked in from the back, and he gestured to me. "Mom, this lady is here to see you. I'm looking up properties for her."

I could see the resemblance between mother and son—both shared the same chestnut brown hair color and deep-tanned skin.

"Thanks, Cody." Suzanne smiled, but looked confused. "Hello. I'm sorry—have we met before? I'm generally good with names."

I took a step closer. "We haven't been introduced yet. I'm Macy Hatfield—my brother and I run the Barks & Beans Cafe just up the street."

Cody piped up. "I've been in there a couple of times. Best coffee in these parts."

My heart warmed. "Thank you. My brother's in charge of ordering the beans, and he gets them from a friend in Costa Rica." Turning back to Suzanne, I said, "We'd discussed opening another branch of the cafe, and I thought I'd pop in and check with you, since I know you all have been here for awhile, so I figured you'd understand what we wanted."

"I opened the office when Cody was just a baby." Suzanne was clearly proud of her business. "We've been here for over thirty years. Now Cody's a co-owner."

"Thirty years..." I pretended to look thoughtful. "You know, my neighbor Vera Cox has been here a long time, too, and she just had a shock from something that happened back in 1989. Did you hear about the bones they found in that house that's getting renovated?"

Suzanne's eyes grew brighter and she nodded. "Oh, honey. I knew that poor woman. Her name was Delta

Buckner, God bless her." She gestured to a cushy armchair. "Have a seat. Yes, I know Vera well—she bought her house through us, actually. Vera and I were both at the baby shower that Delta went missing from—Chrissy Evans was the expecting mother, and she worked as a secretary for me at the time."

I hadn't been aware of that fact. Suzanne seemed eager to talk, so I needed to choose my questions carefully in order to mine any relevant information from her.

"Vera and I spoke about that day a little," I said. "You'd think Delta would've been acting weird at the shower if she felt her life were in some kind of danger." Hopefully, Suzanne would take the bait and fill in the blanks.

"You know, I've thought over that day so many times, but I don't recall her saying anything strange or acting any different than normal. It's true that her marriage wasn't the best. I worked with Billy some, since he was an appraiser, and let's just say that Delta sounded really high-maintenance. I think he never felt like he earned enough to make her happy. They didn't have any kids, though, which was a mercy, I suppose."

"She was best friends with Chrissy, wasn't she?"

"Oh, yes. They went way back. Chrissy had a great marriage, and she couldn't wait to have her baby—it turned out to be a girl she named Samantha. They all live down in Tennessee now. Dale, Chrissy's husband, moved them down there to be closer to his family. He's an accountant—actually helped me set up my business in 1987."

Cody interrupted. "Excuse me, but I've found some properties you might be interested in, Miss Hatfield."

I needed to buy more time to talk with Suzanne, who'd

proved to be quite informative. "Could you print those out? Then I can take my time looking over them."

"Of course." He pressed a couple of buttons, and the printer whirred to life.

"Do you keep in touch with Chrissy?" I asked Suzanne.

"Not really, but I know she visits the area occasionally. Linnie Hancock—that's her mother—lives in the Lilac Terrace nursing home in town." She smiled. "She's ninety years old, but sharp as a tack."

I tried to ease into the topic of where Delta's body was found. "I thought I'd seen somewhere that the house where they dug up Delta's bones had been listed with your realty company. Were you actively showing the place when Delta was buried in the basement?"

Suzanne gave a slow nod. "We were, and, like I told the police, I honestly can't think of any way someone could've gotten in. We had one key for the place, and it was kept locked up here at the agency. I only had two other employees—Chrissy the secretary, and Leslie Sims, who was the agent showing that house."

Seizing on the new information, I asked, "Does Leslie still live here?"

She rolled her eyes and gave a dismissive wave. "Oh, no. I wound up letting her go. Turned out, she wasn't doing much showing at all. In fact, I think that's why that house sat vacant for so long. That, and the fact the place was overpriced. I finally managed to talk the owner into dropping the price in late 1990, then it finally sold in 1991 to an older woman. She updated the place before moving in." She cringed. "I guess she didn't touch the basement, though."

"How could Leslie have missed a dug-up area in the basement? Surely she checked on the place to tidy up before whatever showing she *did* do?"

"That's what I asked myself when they announced the discovery of Delta's body. How could Leslie have missed it? But I'm quite sure it's because she was no good at her job. I'd hired her fresh out of college, and she was the sort who didn't really want to work. She had higher aspirations—to be a model, I think."

"Did she go on to become one after you let her go, do you know?"

She shrugged. "I didn't keep up with her at all. I sent her final paycheck to the address she'd given me in Iowa, and it came back—returned to sender."

"You don't think Leslie had something to do with Delta's murder, do you?" I asked.

"Oh, no. She wouldn't have had any reason to come into contact with her, much less kill her. She wasn't the type who could do something as calculated as hide a body...she was scatterbrained and not much of a go-getter, like you have to be to succeed in realty."

Cody walked over and handed me a sheaf of papers. "Sorry to interrupt," he said quietly. "I think the one on the top might be the best fit for a new cafe."

I smiled. "Thanks so much for all your time. I'll show these to my brother and get back to you if we're interested in anything." As he walked back to his desk, I turned back to Suzanne. "What do *you* think happened to Delta? I'm sure you have some ideas."

She pondered for a moment. "Well, honestly, I don't know. Delta didn't have an outside job, so there weren't any coworkers who might've disliked her. She did well selling Tupperware—she was always having parties. I still have some things I bought from her, although I don't use them anymore. But I didn't know anyone who would've had an ax to grind with her. Like I said, she was a bit froufrou in her tastes, and she did talk down to Billy sometimes. I think she had a temper, because he told me he stayed out of her way when she got angry."

This was a different picture of Delta that was emerging...had she actually been verbally abusive toward her husband? Maybe he'd gotten tired of being her whipping boy and decided to get rid of his tormenter.

A woman walked in the front door, and Suzanne turned to welcome her.

I'd taken up enough of her time. "I'm sorry for keeping you," I said, shifting the pile of papers under my arm as I stood. "I'll definitely let you know if we want to check out any of these properties. Thanks so much."

Suzanne shook my hand. "Please tell Vera hello from me. She always was such a kind person. And Athaleen was your great-aunt, wasn't she?"

When I nodded, Suzanne grinned. "She was the first one we turned to when crises hit the community. She'd pitch in and give it her all. In fact, she organized meals for Billy after Delta went missing, even though the police considered him a suspect. She said pish-posh on it and declared that the poor man needed to keep his strength up. I think she felt Delta had abandoned him—she told me as much."

That threw a different light on things. Much as I wanted to consider Billy a suspect, if Auntie A had liked him, she must have truly believed he didn't harm his wife. She'd always been a good judge of character. If only I'd listened when she'd voiced misgivings about Jake before I married him.

"Thanks for sharing that with me." After a final wave, I opened the door and stepped out into the bright sunlight. I pulled out my phone to call Harper. Maybe we could get together so I could go over what I'd learned and discuss which direction to look next.

6

Harper was working late Saturday night, but she suggested we have pizza on Sunday night instead. I asked her to come over to my place, since I knew she seemed to genuinely enjoy her time with Coal, and she was happy to oblige.

As usual, Bo and I spent Sunday morning together at church, then I had lunch at his place afterward. He'd made a ham, so I brought green beans and salad to go along with it. Summer was busy with a couple of strays that animal control had picked up, so we went ahead and ate without her.

When Bo asked how Harper's house flip was coming along, I told him it was slow going. I didn't fill him in on our little side hunt for Delta's murderer. After all, the case was colder than frost on an iceberg, so I probably wouldn't need his help with it.

But, as usual, my big brother was far more perceptive than I thought. As he loaded the dishwasher, he said, "At

our barbeque, you mentioned you wanted to talk with
Mercer about Delta Buckner's death...did you ever visit
him?"

Reluctantly, I caught him up on my visit with the
retired detective, but he didn't seem all too shocked to
discover Harper and I were poking around into Delta's
murder. In fact, he'd probably guessed that was how I was
spending my free hours.

"Just be careful, sis. Although it's unlikely you'll dig up
something new in the case, since Delta's killer could've
moved to another state or even died by now, you need to
tread lightly. After all, she lived in this town, and so do we. I
don't want you becoming a target for a local wacko."

As I sliced the ham before bagging it up, I considered
Bo's warning. While it was possible Harper and I could kick
over some kind of long-dormant hornet's nest, I doubted it.
So far, we hadn't stumbled onto anything the police were
unaware of.

I supposed that in time, media interest in the gruesome
discovery in Harper's renovated house would die down. Yet
I could understand her desire to get closure on Delta's
death. Rumors might start circulating that the house was
haunted, which would dampen interest. Folks in these parts
had a healthy fear of ghosts.

By extension, people might start avoiding our block and
even our cafe. No, I needed to take one for the team and
keep up my inquiries a little longer. I had the strangest
feeling we were getting close to a breakthrough, even
though that made no sense, given the limited information I'd
acquired.

COAL GREETED Harper with an enthusiastic nose-bump when I opened the door for her. She was toting two pizza boxes, and they smelled amazing.

"I brought a pepperoni and a supreme—hope that's okay," she said. "Sorry I didn't get to touch base first. Once again, my contractor ran into issues with the house—he discovered the wiring was bad on the back wall in the kitchen, so we'll have to redo it."

"I'm sorry to hear that. But supreme is my favorite, so you did great." As I arranged the pizza on the counter next to the veggies and dip I'd prepared, I told her what I'd learned from Suzanne.

Coal sidled up next to Harper's legs and gave her the most pathetic, please-pet-me look. She grinned and patted his head. "What a good boy." As she stood to get a plate, Coal dutifully lumbered over to his pillow in the living room, as if avoiding the pizza temptation.

Once we'd sat down with our food, Harper gave me a thoughtful look. "What about that realtor, Leslie...Sims, was it? She was showing the house at the time, so it seems like she would've noticed *something*, even if she were the most unobservant person in the world."

"That's what I thought, but Suzanne said she doesn't know where she is now. She said she sent a final paycheck to an address in Iowa, but it was returned."

"You can find a lot on the internet these days," Harper said. "I'll check into Leslie; see if I can find her."

"Okay." I grabbed a carrot, plunging it into the dip I'd

piled on my plate. "I'm planning to visit Chrissy's mom in the nursing home—her name is Linnie," I explained. "I can go tomorrow afternoon, after work. The place isn't far away. Maybe she'll remember something."

Harper took a sip of lemonade. "What are your thoughts on Billy Buckner? Mercer told you he seemed to be hiding something."

"I have mixed feelings about Billy. I found it interesting that Suzanne had worked with him when he was an appraiser. She got the impression his wife was demanding. Maybe he didn't earn enough to keep her happy and got sick of trying to please her. But then again, my great-aunt took food to him when Delta went missing, and I seriously doubt she'd do that for someone she suspected of getting rid of his wife."

Harper polished off her slice of pepperoni pizza and wiped her mouth. "That's a reasonable assumption. I'm sure the police have thoroughly investigated Billy by this point. Let's focus on others who knew her for now."

As I gathered up our paper plates, I figured it was as good a time as any to get to know Harper better. She struck me as a woman who didn't have many friends, although I wasn't sure how I'd gotten that impression. "So, have you been flipping houses for long?"

She tugged a hair elastic from her wrist and pulled her long hair up into a bun. As she secured it in place, her white streak gleamed under the kitchen light.

"It's been a couple of years now. I moved to Bath County in Virginia and started fixing up my own older home. Then I was presented with the opportunity to flip a local historical house, and it kind of snowballed from there."

"What did you do before that?" Surely she'd had a career before house-flipping.

Her eyes held mine. "I don't normally share this information, but I believe I can trust you with it. I worked in the Secret Service. After spending many years on Presidential protection detail, I shifted into a role as interrogator."

"As in, you gave polygraphs and things like that?"

"Sort of. I was basically a human lie detector, and I used polygraphs as I did my work."

What a windfall. Now all we needed to do was get Harper around Delta's murderer, and she could tell if the person was lying to us.

She grinned. "I can practically see your wheels spinning, Macy. Yes, I'm very good at spotting liars—for instance, I knew right away that you and your brother are very honest people. But I don't just walk into my interviews blind—it takes some one-on-one time with a suspect to establish a kind of baseline, especially without a polygraph."

"Oh, sure," I said, as if I were an old hand at lie detection.

"But I'll be listening carefully when I talk with Leslie. Your impressions of people inform me, too."

I sat down on the couch and motioned for her to join me. Coal came over and gave me a hopeful look, so I rubbed his ears and face.

"I'm not the best at recognizing liars," I admitted. "My ex-husband really pulled the wool over my eyes."

I wondered if Harper had ever been married—if so, she likely wasn't now, since she wore no ring and she'd never spoken of a husband.

She crossed one leg over the other and tucked a foot on the couch, like a pretzel. "Some guys are really good at that. They become pros at lying, even in their formative years. It's easy for honest people to fall for what they say. But I'm betting you're much savvier now."

"True—I try to go into new relationships with a healthy dose of suspicion."

She nodded. "And your brother told me about his work with the DEA—I'm sure he has your back, too."

Bo had *always* had my back. I'd just chosen not to listen to him, to my own detriment.

"Maybe Billy Buckner is one of those skilled liar types," I said. "Maybe he's just been pretending to be worried about Delta's whereabouts all these years."

She shook her head. "I don't think so. Remember how he gave Mercer mixed signals in those initial interviews, even acting a bit suspicious? If he were a natural liar, he never would've slipped. I wouldn't rule him out, but I think checking into the avenues the police might've overlooked would be the best plan for now."

"How long until your house here will be ready to go on the market, do you think?"

She sighed. "It's hard to tell, but they're estimating four more weeks."

It wasn't a lot of time, especially since Harper and I worked during the days. But there was still an outside chance that we'd turn up something new while talking with people who had known Delta.

As Harper petted Coal with a wistful look in her eyes, I hoped she might run into the perfect shelter dog companion during her morning trips to Barks & Beans. Even if we couldn't resolve Delta's murder before Harper tried to sell her renovated house, at the very least, maybe she'd wind up with a new friend to take home to Virginia.

7

FROM THE MOMENT I stepped into work Monday morning, the cafe was hopping. Summer had brought in three weaned puppies from a litter discovered near the dump, and the tawny fluff-balls tumbled around from one chew toy to the next. Parents on their lunch breaks peppered me with questions about the pups, probably considering them for their children who were still in school.

By the time I handed the Barks section over to Bristol, my go-to dog whispering employee, I was ready to call it a day. After grabbing an iced caramel latte for myself and a Monte Cristo ham sandwich for Linnie, I headed home.

While Coal took his bathroom break, I rummaged around in my cabinets until I turned up an empty glass bottle that would make a good vase. Then I headed out to the garden, snipping three of Auntie A's prized deep purple irises to take to Linnie in the nursing home. I figured flowers and a delicious sandwich could only smooth the way for me to ask a few questions. On top of that, Linnie would have known Auntie A, so that would offer me another "in" when I spoke to her.

THE LILAC TERRACE nursing home proved to be a sprawling place that was, indeed, surrounded by lavender lilac bushes. At the front desk, the secretary gushed about my irises and was only too happy to point me to Linnie Hancock's room.

As I walked down the long hallway, an older woman bustled out of a room. When she adjusted her Seventies-era glasses and pinned me with a look, I recognized too late that I was headed straight toward Matilda Crump, the town busybody.

"Why, Macy Hatfield, I didn't know you were acquainted with anyone at Lilac Terrace," she observed.

Two could play at the nosy game. Instead of enlightening her as to why I was there, I said, "And I didn't realize you knew someone here."

She sniffed. "Widower Joshua Martin had to move in a month ago. I've been dropping by on his daughter's behalf to see that he's being treated with appropriate respect. After all, he was a town councilman for many years."

I nodded. "Impressive. How kind of you to look after him." I wondered if Matilda had any romantic designs on the poor widower, but I'd been to her large, well-furnished house, and I hadn't gotten the impression she was on the prowl. Maybe she was actually just doing a good deed for Joshua's daughter.

I was about to take my leave when Matilda clutched my

arm in her claw-like grip. Dropping her voice, she said, "I was gobsmacked to learn they'd found Delta Buckner's body in that house across from your cafe. Coshed in the head, they said. Still, one must sleep in the bed one makes for oneself, I suppose."

Extricating my arm from her hand, I said, "What do you mean? Surely she didn't deserve to be killed!"

"Oh, simmer down, my dear. Nothing like that. It's just that Delta flew against her parents' advice when she married that William Sylvester—Billy, as they call him— knowing full well he was a bad boy. He pinched things as a teen, stealing from local shops and the like." Her faux-British accent kicked in as her voice grew louder. "Though truly, it shouldn't have come as any surprise when Delta started selling that Tupperware and painting herself up to go flirting around town. It didn't slow her down a bit if a man happened to be married. Why, the vixen even tried to chat up my husband Miles, if you could believe it. She had no boundaries."

"You don't say." I'd dropped my voice to a near-whisper, hoping she'd lower hers to match mine.

But Matilda just rolled right along at top volume. "I think she was even talking with Chrissy's husband Dale on the day of the baby shower. Dale was the handsomest man in Lewisburg at the time, but he only had eyes for his wife, bless him. Their happy marriage seemed straight out of a fairy tale."

Matilda had actually provided me with an interesting new angle on the dynamics of Delta's friend group. "But she and Chrissy were best friends, right? Wouldn't Chrissy have noticed if Delta flirted with her husband?"

"Oh, Delta only cornered men when they were alone, like she did to my Miles. I daresay she knew she had no chance with Dale, but it was just like her to give it the old college try." She glanced at the bottle of irises in my hand. "But don't let me keep you from going to see..."

Her voice trailed off, and I knew she was waiting for me to fill in the blank. Much as I perversely wanted to leave her hanging, she *had* done right by me today by giving me the unvarnished truth about Delta. "I'm here to check in on Linnie Hancock, actually," I explained.

Her eyes actually seemed to soften behind the thick lenses of her glasses. "Why, Linnie's an absolute angel. She welcomed me into the church family and got me involved in the garden club. Please tell her hello from me."

I was surprised to see someone as prickly as Matilda showing any true fondness for anyone, although she was a human being like anyone else. "Will do."

As she clomped off toward the entrance in her practical, thick-soled shoes, I headed the other way until I reached Linnie's door. I gave it a firm rap.

A faint voice answered, "Come in."

I opened the door and glanced around the private bedroom. It appeared to have an attached bathroom with a walk-in shower, which made it feel more spacious. Linnie was sitting in a comfortable chair right next to a window. I could see a bird feeder just outside, where a cardinal was pecking away at seed.

"Such a lovely day out, isn't it?" she asked, clearly unconcerned as to who I was or why I was in her room.

"A perfect spring day." I situated the flower bottle on a rolling table in her line of vision. "I'm Macy Hatfield—you knew my great-aunt Athaleen. I brought you some of her irises and a sandwich from the cafe my brother and I run."

Linnie beamed a smile at me. "Athaleen was one of my dearest friends. How delightful to see her irises again! She always grew the biggest and healthiest flowers—I'm convinced the secret was in the fertilizer she got from a farmer friend." Her eyes shifted to the sandwich bag. "And a sandwich! I'll enjoy that for my supper. Would you mind putting it in my little fridge in the corner? Then you can come and have a seat with me." She patted the bed next to her.

After sliding the bag into the fridge, I sat down and observed Linnie, finding it hard to believe the elegant woman was ninety. She wore well-tailored pants and a beautiful cornflower blue cardigan that brought out her eyes. Her thick platinum hair was cut in a modern style, and her pink nails had been recently manicured. It was good to see she was doing so well. But I needed to get down to business.

"I came here today hoping you might shed a little light on things," I began. "I've talked with my neighbor, Vera Cox, about Chrissy's shower, but I thought maybe you'd noticed something she'd overlooked."

A grin spread across Linnie's lips. "Vera isn't the most detail-oriented person. But she's a sweetie—she checks in on me nearly every month. What were you specifically wondering about, dear?"

"Well, I was interested to know what your daughter thought when she heard the news of her best friend's murder. She's living in Tennessee now, is that right?"

Linnie nodded. "They moved down to be near Dale's

father before he died, then they just stayed there. But Chrissy drives up all the time to visit me. They have children now, and I have five great-grandchildren." She gestured to a bulletin board filled with letters and cards. "I'm spoiled with having such a wonderful family. Not everyone my age has that kind of blessing."

She crossed her legs as her gaze turned serious. "It was a shock for Chrissy, for sure. For all those years, no one saw hide nor hair of Delta. Then the police called Chrissy with news of Delta's body. First thing she did was call me, then Billy. She was worried how he'd take it. Do you know that for all these years, Chrissy has sent him a card on the anniversary of her baby shower, just to let him know she still misses Delta, too."

I pounced on this information. "Chrissy didn't believe that Billy had harmed Delta?"

Her lips tightened, as if she were considering the right way to word things. "Delta had...a rough upbringing, to put it mildly. She'd always wanted to move away; go somewhere glitzy like Vegas. But then she settled for Billy, who wasn't known as the most law-abiding kid. We all knew that boy would never leave West Virginia, but for some reason, she got hitched to him. Chrissy always guessed that Delta walked away that day to follow her dreams elsewhere. So yes, her death came as a shock."

"You were at the shower," I said. "Did you see anyone acting strangely toward Delta, or did anything unusual happen?"

Linnie shook her head. "It was just like any other baby shower." She leaned back in her chair, pressing her fingers together. "Let me think what ladies attended. There was

Suzanne Payette—Dale had helped her get her realty business going, and it was starting to do well, I believe. Vera had small children then, and your aunt Athaleen kept busy raising you two young whippersnappers." She winked. "The pastor's wife was there—she's in an assisted living home now. And Diana's died. Oh, and Matilda Crump was there. She had no children, of course, and she hadn't been in town long when Delta went missing. They moved away not long after."

I recalled Matilda's greeting. "She said to tell you hello, by the way."

Linnie's aristocratic nose wrinkled almost imperceptibly, but she maintained her manners. "How sweet. Tell her hello back."

A care assistant entered, carrying afternoon medicines for Linnie. In case Linnie was more forgetful than she seemed, I let the assistant know I'd placed a sandwich in the fridge for her. Then I stood and placed a hand on Linnie's thin one.

"Thank you so much for letting me visit today," I said. "It's been wonderful to chat with you."

Linnie smiled. "I hope I've been of some help to you, dear. And I've heard so much about your cafe. Your auntie would be so proud of you. She always said you and Bo belonged here in West Virginia—near your Hatfield roots. I'm so glad you moved back."

I gave her a warm hug and headed out. I hadn't really learned anything new, but Linnie was certainly the kind of person who made everyone feel welcome—even Matilda. I appreciated that she hadn't asked me why I was interested in Delta's murder investigation, so there'd been no need to explain myself.

If I didn't stumble onto some clue as to the day Delta went missing, I might have to call it quits on the investigation, and I hated to do that to Harper. We hadn't talked with Chrissy or Billy yet, so maybe I could ask Detective Hatcher for their numbers. I hated that every trail I'd gone down had proved to be a dead end, but I supposed that was par for the course with a murder that had happened decades ago.

8

COAL WAS anxious for some exercise when I arrived home, so I leashed him, then led him along the sidewalk toward Bo's place. My brother's kitchen light was on, so he was probably eating supper or unwinding after his daily jog. I decided to let him relax.

As I was crossing the street to extend our walk, Harper called. "Hey, Macy. How'd it go with Linnie today?"

I filled her in on what the older lady had told me. "I think she and Chrissy always believed that Delta took off and left Billy. Sounds like Delta despised living here and wanted to get out."

"Well, I think I found something." Harper's tone was energized. "I got hold of Leslie, if you can believe it. I had a friend track her down."

I stopped short, so Coal halted in front of me, giving me what could only be described as a quizzical look. "What did she say?" I asked.

"That she was actually fired for asking too many questions. Robbins Realty was a small firm, but Suzanne drove a high-end Cadillac, routinely bought designer handbags and shoes, and owned a huge house. One time, Leslie jokingly asked her if her ex was wealthy. She was fired the next day. Suzanne then threatened that she wouldn't give Leslie a referral unless she moved out of the southern West Virginia area."

"That's odd—why would she say that area specifically?"

"Leslie guessed it was because that's where all her realty contacts were, but she wasn't sure. Anyway, you know how Suzanne said she'd sent that final paycheck to Iowa? She did no such thing. Leslie was living at that address for ten years."

"So Suzanne lied to me," I said.

"And to the police, I'm sure," Harper continued. "Leslie repeatedly called Robbins Realty, but they hung up on her. She finally came to the conclusion that something crooked was going on with the business, but she could never figure out what. She did say that Billy Buckner hung around after hours sometimes, so she wondered if he and Suzanne were having an affair."

I considered that angle. "It's definitely possible, since they worked closely with each other. But then again..." Something wasn't sitting right with me. "Maybe it was a business thing. Billy was an appraiser. Would there be any way he and Suzanne could've been in cahoots, financially speaking?" Coal gave a subtle but impatient tug on his leash, so I started another loop around the block.

Harper gasped. "I'll bet that's it! It's common knowledge in the realty industry that appraisers sometimes inflate home values—a form of mortgage fraud—and it's considered a white-collar crime. Billy could've been inflating the value of the homes Suzanne was selling. Maybe even the house I have now, come to think of it."

"That would explain why it sat empty so long," I said. "And it might also explain why Billy seemed shifty to Mercer. He could have been hiding something that could land him in prison. I think I'll pay Suzanne a little visit on my lunch break tomorrow, maybe ask some pointed questions about Billy's appraisal work. I'll watch her reactions."

"That might not be wise," Harper said. "Listen, I really appreciate all your help trying to clear the air about Delta's murder so I can sell the house, but I don't want you doing anything dangerous. If Suzanne was involved in a scam with Billy, she's not going to appreciate your questions."

I chuckled. "Are you hinting that she'd try to attack me? You don't have to worry. I'm 5'3, and she's shorter and built like a twig. In fact, I could knock her over if I wanted. But I'll take my pepper spray, if that'll make you feel better."

"Thanks. Just be careful. If she starts acting strangely, get out of there and call Detective Hatcher."

I grinned. Harper sounded just like Bo. But I was old enough to take care of myself. "Okay. Also, I was planning to ask the detective for Billy and Chrissy's numbers so we could talk to them. Would you want to call them after work sometime? I was just thinking that you *are* the human lie detector and all that, so you might pick up on something I wouldn't."

Harper laughed. "Sure. Leave it to me. But right now I need to give my investor a call and fill him in on our house progress—such as it is. Thanks for checking into Suzanne's story, Macy. If that doesn't pan out and my calls to Chrissy and Billy are fruitless, I think we've exhausted all our options. I just won't tell potential buyers about the body in the basement."

"Nice try, but you're underestimating how fast the word spreads in a small town like this. I guarantee you that anyone from this area or the neighboring counties already knows the grisly story of the bones."

She sighed. "Sometimes there's nowhere to go but forward. We'll just have to buckle up and plunge ahead, full-force."

As we arrived home, Coal gave a little leap, ready to give his garden a thorough sniff-down. I opened the gate, unhooking his leash so he could roam the yard. "Let's touch base tomorrow night," I told Harper.

Hopefully, at that point, we'd have something of relevance to share.

SUMMER SHOWED up soon after I'd unlocked the cafe on Tuesday morning. The moment I clapped eyes on the bigger of the two dogs she'd brought over, I let out an excited whoop.

"What's up?" She glanced down at the German Shepherd mix. "I promise she's a sweetie, even though she looks tough."

"She might be perfect for Harper," I said. "Her German Shepherd died, and I'm guessing she'd like a dog that looks similar."

Summer walked the dogs into the Barks section and

unleashed them. "Possibly, although sometimes bereaved owners want something totally different."

"It's worth introducing them, I think." I threw another glance at the tan-coated, muscular-looking dog. "How'd you get this one?" I didn't stretch out a hand to pet her, since I liked to give the shelter animals time to adjust to their new environment.

"It was one of those unusual cases. There's an older lady who was breeding Akitas with German Shepherds—they're called 'Shepkitas'—and she found out she needed surgery on her arm. She knew she couldn't manage walking the bigger dogs, like she'd planned. She sold all of them except this girl. Her name is Clementine."

I looked into the dog's rich brown eyes. The black Shepherd markings stood out on her otherwise tan face, giving her a kind of raised-eyebrow look, as if she were begging for love.

"Is she fully grown? How's her temperament?"

"The lady said she's almost two now. She said Clementine has a couple of quirks, but nothing worrisome. So far, I haven't noticed anything unusual. She eats well, she's super docile, and she isn't aggressive with the other dogs."

"I'll keep an eye on her today and see if she might be a good match. Harper hasn't eaten breakfast at the cafe lately —I figure she's making coffee at home and getting straight to work, now that construction is fully underway."

"She seems like a really driven person," Summer said. "Have you had any luck looking into Delta Buckner's murder? Find out anything interesting?"

"Not really." I tossed a ball to Clementine. She grabbed

it, then graciously nudged it toward the smaller dog, probably hoping to play.

"It's almost always the husband or boyfriend." Summer flipped her ponytail and gave me a wise look. "Haven't you listened to any of those true crime podcasts?"

"They're too gruesome for me. But yes, I realize that. Harper's going to be talking with Billy Buckner very soon, I hope."

"Should be easy since he's moved back into their old house," Summer said.

Goosebumps ran up my arms. "Wait—what are you talking about?"

"You know how the Buckners lived a couple of houses down from the place Harper's renovating? One of my shelter employees rents an apartment next to the Buckner place. He said he recognized Billy Buckner from the news, and he was moving boxes into that house."

I couldn't believe it. "After all these years, he's come back to town?" I asked.

"The house has never had a For Sale sign up, so I'm guessing Billy's held onto it all these years."

I tried to process this news. Billy Buckner was now within walking distance of the cafe, and even closer to Harper as she renovated the house. Given the off chance he had killed Delta, it wasn't a comforting thought.

"Maybe he's just moving things out—maybe even Delta's things," I said. "Now that he knows she's gone, he might want to sell the place." I envisioned boxes of unsold Tupperware products crowded into a closet.

"Sure...I guess my employee could've gotten it wrong

and Billy was moving the boxes out." Summer could probably tell I wasn't happy with this new development.

As she headed back to the shelter, I considered my options. Although I could walk down to the Buckner house and see what Billy was up to, that would be a little too obvious.

Instead, I texted Harper to give her a heads-up. While it was unlikely that Billy would drop by her house, especially when renovations were underway, she needed to be aware he was around. On the off chance he'd killed his wife, he might have some reason to revisit the site where he'd buried her.

Shoving thoughts of Billy aside, I came up with a few questions I could ask Suzanne on my lunch break. Until I had a chance to follow up with her, I was running on fumes of suspicion that weren't even strong enough to smell.

9

For lunch, I asked Kylie, my tattooed barista with a heart of gold, to make me a maple latte to go. I planned to grab one of Charity's grilled chicken pesto sandwiches when I got back from my self-assigned lunchtime task.

The sky was a deep, cloudless blue as I walked up to Robbins Realty, coffee cup in hand and pepper spray in my pocket. I'd looked over the properties Cody had printed out, so I was ready with my real estate inquiries. Although we weren't really planning to buy property now, at least I'd have a better idea about what they would cost if and when we did open a satellite branch of the cafe.

Once again, Cody was seated behind the desk as I walked in, and he stood to greet me. "I'm so glad you've returned," he said. "What did you think of those properties?"

I glanced around, but Suzanne wasn't in sight. "I had some thoughts, but wondered if I could chat with your mom really quickly first?"

He looked apologetic. "I'm sorry, but she's out on her

lunch break. I'm happy to field any questions you might have."

I hesitated. Cody had only been a small child when Delta was murdered, but he must've had some contact with Billy as he grew older.

"I was just looking into William Sylvester Buckner. Do you know him?"

One of his eyebrows raised. "You mean Billy? Sure. He worked some with my mom, back when he lived in this area."

"I've heard he's back in Lewisburg," I said. "Has he dropped in at all?"

Cody looked a little worried. "I had no idea he was in town. I'll let Mom know."

I wasn't sure if I should voice my suspicions to Cody, especially since they involved his mother's possible involvement in a real estate scheme. But he cleared the path for me.

"Why are you asking about him? Is there something we need to be aware of?"

I took a breath before plunging in. "I was thinking about how Billy worked as an appraiser for years. My friend mentioned that sometimes appraisers can inflate home values, which is considered mortgage fraud. I wondered if Billy could've been involved in something like that at the time his wife was murdered, which might be a link to her death. I thought your mom might have some insights on it."

Cody looked horrified. "I can't imagine Mom would've worked with someone who was dishonest like that. She has very high standards."

Trying to smooth his ruffled feathers, I said, "I'm sure

your mom knew nothing about it. I just wanted to talk with her before I suggested that the police look into Billy's business dealings back in 1989."

Cody seemed more disturbed than I'd thought he would be. "I'm sure Mom had nothing to do with any realty scam," he insisted. "Tell you what—I'll try to find our sales files from that time. Maybe we kept something that will help the police. Could you hang on a second?"

The clock on the wall said I had forty minutes of lunch break left. "Sure. I'm not in a rush."

I took a seat as Cody walked into a back room. Glancing toward the front window, I was disappointed to find there wasn't much of a view. Low shutters blocked the sidewalk from my angle, although I was able to make out the tops of heads as people passed by.

After a few moments, Cody stepped out of the room, folders in hand. His eyes registered obvious distress as he said, "You might want to look at this."

I walked closer, reaching for the files he extended. But before I could grab them, they slid from his hand to the floor. He heaved a sigh.

I hurried to pick them up, but when I stood to face him, a surge of fear raced through me.

Cody had a pair of sharp scissors pointed toward my heart.

"Billy was crooked," he calmly explained. "But so was my mother. So you'll understand why I can't allow the police to start poking around in her past. Besides, as soon as Delta went missing, Billy got cold feet and backed out of working with Mom. Our company took a hit, but Mom managed to stay afloat. So you see, it's all in the past, and that's where it's going to stay."

I tried to keep my breathing steady. My pepper spray was in my pocket, but I was holding the sheaf of folders in my hands, and he'd definitely notice if I made any sudden moves. I wasn't convinced I could beat him to the draw. If I could only keep him talking until his mom returned, she'd surely put a stop to things. "What do you care about all this? If it's long over and done, there's nothing for you to worry about."

He cleared his throat. "Well, it's not *completely* done, actually. I've decided to carry the family torch, so to speak. Mom doesn't know. I couldn't find an appraiser to suit my purposes, but I did find a home inspector who's more than happy to say things are better than they actually are. It's a long-view scam, but it does pad the paycheck, so to speak."

I took a step backward, hoping to make a break for the door. But Cody took two steps closer, so the sharp blades hovered dangerously close to my chest. I could only hope and pray his mom would walk in.

"But you didn't kill Delta—you were just a kid," I said. "How does she play into things? Did Billy kill her?"

"I have no idea. He could have, although he always seemed more the spineless, grumbling type to me." He gave an annoyed grunt. "All I know is that you can't direct your police friends to our records. I wish I could trust you to keep quiet about things, but that's not likely." He gestured to the back door. "Now let's head that way, out to my car. I can't do this in here."

As he moved behind me and the tips of the scissors poked into my back, I subtly shifted the folders into my left hand. I pretended to stumble forward, hunching over a bit as I slipped my pepper spray from my right pocket into my palm.

"S-sorry," I said. Before he could respond, I whipped around, aiming a liberal stream directly into his eyes.

With a screech, he dropped the scissors. He fumbled in a blind attempt to grab me, but I was already racing toward the door. Once I got outside, I took off running toward the left, and I kept going until I reached the house where Harper was renting the downstairs floor.

Panting, I dashed around back where I couldn't be seen and called Charlie Hatcher. After giving him the news of my near-deadly run-in with Cody, he assured me he'd be on his way, with backup. "Stay right where you are, out of sight," he instructed.

My hand was shaking as I clung to my phone like a lifeline. Although I found it difficult to believe Cody would stab me to death just to cover up his real estate fraud, I knew people would go to incredible lengths to hide their dirty secrets. I'd certainly learned that over the years.

My phone rang. Harper's voice sounded in my ear.

"Macy, I saw you run past my porch—what's going on?"

"How did you see me? Are you home?"

"No—I'm at work. But I've installed a security camera on my front door that feeds into a phone app."

Of course she had. I quickly explained my horrific encounter at Robbins Realty. I could hear movement in the background, like Harper's phone was shaking. "I'm on my way over there," she said.

"Over where?" I demanded. Did she mean here or the realty office?

"I'm closer than the police. I'll make sure Cody doesn't go anywhere. I'm trained to lock down situations like this."

I didn't ask if Harper had a weapon—something told me she didn't even need one.

I peeked around the side of the house, but saw only a few pedestrians meandering a little way up the street from Robbins Realty. Cody was nowhere to be seen.

Suddenly, Harper rounded a sidewalk, running at top speed until she reached the realty office. She banged on the front door. When no one answered, she tried the knob, but it appeared to have been locked. Without hesitation, she leaped over the porch and jogged over to a side window. It didn't take long until she was crawling into the house.

No more than three minutes later, police cars circled the driveway and sidewalks, blocking any escape route. The front door opened, and Cody stumbled onto the porch. He was still wiping at his eyes, which looked puffy and red even from this distance. Harper walked behind him, and she had something pointed at his back. I doubted it was scissors.

Once Detective Hatcher stepped out of his car, I edged out from behind Harper's place and slowly walked toward the realty office. An officer walked over to Cody, snapping handcuffs on him before marching him to a police vehicle, so he was out of the way by the time I reached the porch.

"Thank you, Harper," the detective said as I climbed the stairs. "Nice work."

It was almost like he knew about Harper's previous job, because he didn't bat an eye as she sheathed her pistol in a concealed carry holster in the front of her jeans. Once her shirt fell over it, the gun was basically invisible.

"I always carry it," she explained to me. "It's kind of an extension of myself at this point."

My brother Bo and my FBI boyfriend Titan probably felt the same way about their weapons. It was strange when they weren't carrying one.

I gave Harper a nod. "My pepper spray came in handy today. I'm glad you asked me to take it along."

The detective chuckled. "That's for sure. We'll see to Cody's eye care, but then he's going to answer some questions for me."

"He said he didn't know who killed Delta," I said. "All he admitted was the realty fraud I mentioned to you."

"We'll dig into his story and see if we find out something new." The detective gave us each a quick smile and headed down the stairs.

I looked at Harper. "Thanks again for showing up so quickly. Was Cody hiding when you got into the house?"

Harper's eyes narrowed. "He was upstairs, moaning in the bathroom and trying to rinse the pepper out of his eyes. He was willing enough for me to take him out to meet the police, if that meant someone could relieve his pain."

"Has anyone seen his mom? Cody told me Suzanne was on lunch break. Maybe he told her to get out of town."

She shook her head. "Detective Tucker said they found her at the Chinese restaurant, and she's already been taken down to the station for questioning. You and I are free to get back to work—if you feel up to it, that is."

"I think I am." I managed a grin before checking the time. "Wow, that was a really extended lunch break. Good thing Bo's not working today, or he would've called the moment I didn't show up."

"A protective big brother," she said. "I always wanted one. Hey, how about you come over to my place tonight so we can catch up more—maybe around eight? I was planning to make my favorite turkey burgers."

She didn't have to ask twice. When someone else was willing to cook for me, I was happy to oblige. "Sure. And I'll bring some dessert from the cafe."

10

As I walked over to Harper's place, the sun was slipping below the mountains, sending glowing red and pink ribbons of light across the horizon. I took a deep breath, picking up on the scents of fresh-cut grass and someone grilling nearby. I had escaped being impaled with a pair of scissors, and I felt happy to be alive.

I hadn't told Bo about that little adventure yet.

Harper greeted me warmly and ushered me inside. Her place was sparsely furnished with items that had definitely seen better days.

"Come on into the kitchen," she said. "I have everything ready."

After filling my plate with a burger and potato wedges and grabbing a water bottle, I took a seat at her tiny table. "I have some news," I announced.

She got her food and settled into the chair next to me. "What's up?"

"I found a dog for you."

She grinned. "I'm not so sure about that. I don't even know if I'm ready for another dog after Frida."

I shared about Clementine's visit to the cafe today. "She's what they call a 'Shepkita.'" I pulled out my phone, showing her several photos I'd taken of the dog.

Her gaze softened. "Oh, she's beautiful."

"I paid close attention to her all day," I continued. "Her owner told Summer that she had some quirks, but the only one I noticed was that she got a little nervous when men approached her. Still, she didn't shy away and she didn't get aggressive, like she was ready to bite. Trust me—I know dogs, and I think she'd be a great companion for you."

"Where is she now?" Harper asked.

"Back at the shelter. I gave Summer strict instructions not to adopt her out until you'd had a chance to meet her."

She grinned. "Sounds like I'll be paying a visit to the shelter, then. Thanks for thinking of me, Macy."

"Of course."

I squirted a pile of ketchup onto my burger, then added mayo and lettuce. The moment I bit into it, flavor burst in my mouth. "This is fantastic! My turkey burgers always taste so bland."

"I add a lot of spices—paprika especially." She dipped a potato wedge into ketchup. "I have some good news, too. I have Chrissy Evans' phone number. I thought we could call her tonight and fill her in on what we know. Since she worked at Robbins Realty back in the day, she might have some insight into Billy's dealings with Suzanne."

"Good idea. Have you seen Billy lurking around your reno job?"

"Not at all, and believe me, I have my construction crew

on the lookout. They won't let anyone creep around the place."

"Let's talk to Chrissy, then maybe we could pay a little visit to Billy's house sometime and ask him about his involvement with Suzanne—although I'm sure Detective Hatcher will be looking into that, too."

"The crazy thing is that we're no closer to discovering who killed Delta than we were before. We know Suzanne and Billy were involved in mortgage fraud. We know that Cody has more recently been involved in realty fraud himself. But nothing seems to connect with a motive to kill Delta."

"I agree. Let's chat with Chrissy and see if she can shed any light on things."

AFTER FINISHING off the tiramisu I'd brought, we headed into the living room and sat down on Harper's threadbare floral couch. She called Chrissy's number, then put it on speakerphone.

Chrissy picked up quickly, and Harper explained who we were and why we were calling. She gave a brief rundown of the people we'd spoken to—including her mom—then told Chrissy about my showdown with Cody today.

Chrissy gave a gasp. "It's all true, then," she said.

"What's all true?" I asked.

"Billy and Suzanne were running a con job. I always had a bad feeling about their after-hours meetings. One time, I glanced over a report Billy dropped off. It seemed like some housing values had been altered, but I couldn't be sure because I didn't know enough about it."

"We believe Leslie was let go because she questioned Suzanne about her income source," I said.

"That makes sense. Suzanne fired Leslie out of the clear blue sky without any good reason, although she did accuse her of being lazy." Chrissy took a deep breath. "In fact, after my baby shower, Delta came back into the kitchen to get the dessert I'd set aside for her. I thought it was a good time to bring up Billy's crooked report. She needed to know that her husband might be involved in something illegal with Suzanne."

"And what did she say?" Harper asked.

"Well, she said something about how I should mind my own business and not ruin her husband's career." Chrissy's voice wavered. "She really lost it on me. We were standing in the kitchen..." As her voice trailed off, we heard her give a loud sniff.

Harper shot me a serious look. When she spoke, her tone had shifted into something winsome and almost hypnotic. "Chrissy, what happened in the kitchen?"

Chrissy gave a loud sob. "I can't hold this in anymore. I promised her I would, but I just can't."

Harper's words flowed into Chrissy's pauses like syrup onto a waffle. "You'd feel better if you told someone."

At this point, it dawned on me that Chrissy wasn't just relating any old story to us. She was about to tell us what had really happened to Delta that day.

Her next words were quiet. "Delta got this crazed look in her eyes. She was babbling something about how I could have a baby and she couldn't, and how I thought my husband was so perfect, but I talked bad about hers. She grabbed my cast iron frying pan from the stovetop and swung it upward. I could tell she was about to bring it down on my stomach. I was wedged against the counter, so I couldn't get out of her way." She sniffed. "My mother had just walked in, since she'd heard Delta's tirade. When Mother saw her aiming that pan at me, she grabbed the closest thing she could—my metal teapot—and hit Delta on the head with it."

"She was protecting you," I murmured.

Harper gave a silent nod.

"Exactly. She never meant to kill Delta—just to stop her. But Delta crumpled to the floor right in front of me. Her head was bleeding some, and she...she wasn't breathing anymore."

I felt like we really needed to have Detective Hatcher in on this conversation, but there was no way we could ask Chrissy to pause as she vented a story she'd been sitting on for decades.

"We understand," Harper said. "There was nothing you could do at that point. So you decided to hide her body."

"I'd visited the vacant house Leslie was showing, and I knew it had a dirt basement. It occurred to me that I could take the key from the office and we could hide Delta's body there, since Leslie hadn't had many bites on the place. If we could just get Delta into the ground, I figured the smell of death wouldn't be so bad." Her voice broke. "I know it sounds so calculated, but honestly I was grasping at straws for ways to make such a terrible accident go away. I was about to have a baby."

"Of course you were," Harper said. "So you managed to get her into the ground."

"Mother found a shower curtain for us to wrap her in. It was so much work for us to haul her into the trunk, dig the hole, bury her, then cover her up with that empty chest freezer. Thank goodness Dale was working late like he always did back then. It was such a gamble to leave Delta there, but as the secretary at Robbins Realty, I was able to field calls and watch for when someone showed interest in the house. By some miracle, months passed before anyone asked about it. Before I scheduled Leslie's next showing, I was able to slip in and make sure there was no lingering scent. We'd left the basement windows cracked, and I think that must've helped. It just smelled a little mildewed."

"Your mother has kept this secret all these years," I said. "It must be difficult for her, too."

Chrissy let out another sob. "Mother was the one who told me to keep quiet. She said she didn't want my baby being born in prison. She said we could never tell, as long as we lived."

"She was pretty unruffled when I went to see her. Didn't she worry Billy might be falsely accused of murder?" I asked.

"She knew they wouldn't find a shred of evidence pointing to him. In a way, it was the perfect crime...but it hasn't been perfect for me. Dale could tell you, I've had recurring nightmares about Delta since it happened. But even he doesn't know the real reason why."

Harper spoke firmly. "Do you want to tell Detective Hatcher, or should we?"

Chrissy sounded nervous. "Oh, no. We can't tell. I

promised Mother. And what would my children and grandchildren think if this came out?"

I understood Chrissy's point of view. After all, Linnie was now ninety years old and in a nursing home. Surely she'd committed nothing more than manslaughter, at the most. In a desperate situation, she'd taken action to defend the life of her daughter and her unborn baby.

"I don't know the law in this case, but I have a friend I could speak to about it," Harper said. "Do you want me to talk with him and then let you know how he thinks things would go?"

"Oh, please," Chrissy said. "I would be so happy to get this weight off my shoulders, but I don't want to jeopardize my mother's peace during her later years in life. She can't go to trial at this age."

"I'll let you know," Harper assured her. "Thank you for sharing this with us."

"Yes," I said. "You did the right thing. Billy's been under scrutiny for years, too. I'm sure he'll be glad to finally get the all-clear...although he was mixed up with Suzanne in her realty scheme."

"Oh—I meant to tell you—Billy must've gotten out of that soon after Delta died. He stopped working with Suzanne, and another appraiser stepped in. I assumed it was because the police were going over his life with a fine-tooth comb. I'm not sure if Suzanne continued her con at that point."

"Cody said that his mom got out of it, too." It was ironic that when Delta, who'd defended her husband's shyster ways, had gone missing, both Billy and his partner in crime had abandoned their crooked schemes.

After we said our goodbyes to Chrissy, Harper leaned back on the couch and heaved a huge sigh. "Well, that was crazy."

"I agree. I almost feel like we shouldn't tell the police that Linnie did it. I don't think Poirot would."

Harper chuckled. "It's not quite so easy as that. Sure, Hercule can give a pass to people who took the law into their own hands to rid the world of a thoroughly evil man, but that's just fiction. I'll call my defense lawyer friend tonight. He's one of the best, and he'll let me know how things could go for Linnie."

I thought of the elegant, kind woman I'd met at Lilac Terrace. If there was any justice in this world, she'd be allowed to put this whole thing behind her—and so would her daughter.

11

Three Weeks Later

VERA CALLED me over to her porch as I walked out my gate. "Come and join us, Macy."

Although I'd planned a trip to the grocery store, I'd gladly put it on hold to visit with my neighbor. As I walked toward Vera's yard, I saw that Mercer Priestly was sitting in a white wicker chair next to her. He rocked slowly as he sipped on a glass of sweet iced tea.

"It's the most pleasant June, isn't it?" he asked. "Not too hot. Perfect weather for porch-sitting."

"I agree," I said. "Good to see you, Mercer."

"We were just catching up," Vera said, pouring a glass of tea for me. "How did things turn out for Linnie, do you know?"

"I asked Charlie to update me, but I figure he's been busy with other things this summer," Mercer said.

"The prosecutor dismissed the case," I said. "Chrissy and

Linnie told their story, and since it fit the facts so perfectly, there was no need to look further. In fact, Chrissy handed over Delta's purse as proof, which she'd kept hidden all these years in her attic. It was a case of self-defense, plain and simple—not even manslaughter, which necessitates an overreaction to a threat. Linnie didn't overreact."

"Are they going to splash it all over the news?" Vera twisted her hands together. "I'd hate that for Linnie and her whole family."

"I think it's being dealt with quietly," I said. "It'll be in the news that Delta was killed in self-defense, but Linnie and Chrissy's names won't be brought into it."

Mercer nodded. "It sounds like the best possible outcome of a sad situation. I'm sure Billy will be glad he doesn't have that cloud hanging over him."

"He's finally moving Delta's things out of his old house," I said. "Harper and I dropped in when we saw him on his driveway. We explained who we were." Choking up at the memory, I gave a short cough before continuing my story. "He actually started crying when he thanked us for figuring out what happened to his wife."

Vera placed her hand on mine. "You and Harper did the right thing...and so did Linnie. A mother's love knows no bounds. I would've done the same thing, if someone threatened my daughter and grandbaby."

Knowing Vera's relationship with her own daughter was tenuous for reasons I wasn't privy to, I changed the topic. "Mercer, you'll have to drop into Barks & Beans while you're over here. Bo's working today, and he'd love to see you."

Mercer looked thoughtful. "You know, maybe I will. I could use a good strong cup of coffee."

I glanced toward the sidewalk, and saw Harper walking our way—with her new dog, Clementine. Once she'd petted Clementine at the shelter, it hadn't taken long for her to form a fast bond.

Harper stepped over toward the fence, and Waffles launched into frenzied barking behind the living room window. I was surprised the ditzy Doodle would even notice someone on the sidewalk, but I was glad she'd turned into a good guard dog for Vera.

"I was just sharing with Vera and Mercer how things turned out," I shouted toward Harper. "How's Clementine doing?"

"She's fantastic. I can't wait to get her back to my place in Virginia."

"When are you leaving, dear?" Vera asked.

"Probably tomorrow. The house is finished, and it turned out even better than I'd hoped."

"It's gorgeous," I said. "I love looking out the cafe window at it. It's really raised the bar for the aesthetic of our street."

"Just like your cafe did." Harper smiled. Clementine took a seat at her feet. "I'm taking a little walk, then I need to get back to packing up the few things I brought."

I stood and walked over to her so we could talk more easily. As I gave Clementine a head pat, I asked, "Are you still planning on coming over to Bo's tonight for a little farewell cookout?"

"I wouldn't miss it. You all have kept me caffeinated and fed while I was here, you found me the perfect dog, and you cleared up the mystery around the house I want to sell. I can't thank you enough."

I leaned in and gave Harper a hug. "I'm thankful you came to Lewisburg." As Clementine angled her long ears my way, I added, "And your doggie certainly is, too."

ALSO BY HEATHER DAY GILBERT

Enjoy your visit to the Barks & Beans Cafe?

Read through Books 1-3 in the boxed set collection today, available in Kindle and Kindle Unlimited!

(All individual series titles available in softcover, Kindle, and Kindle Unlimited)

"Intelligent characters, an interesting setting, a wonderful Great Dane"~Cozy up with Kathy blog review

Welcome to the Barks & Beans Cafe, a quaint place where folks pet shelter dogs while enjoying a cup of java...and where murder sometimes pays a visit. Join siblings Macy and Bo Hatfield as they sniff out crimes in their hometown...with plenty of dogs along for the ride!

The Barks & Beans Cafe cozy mystery series features a small town, an amateur sleuth, and no swearing or graphic scenes.

Boxed set includes Books 1-3 in the Barks & Beans Cafe cozy mystery series: NO FILTER, ICED OVER, and FAIR TRADE.

"No Filter checks all my cozy boxes. Wonderful characters, an intriguing mystery, just the right amount of humor and a great big dog named Coal." ~Dollycass Reviews

The Barks & Beans Cafe series in order:

Book 1: No Filter

Book 2: Iced Over

Book 3: Fair Trade

Book 4: Spilled Milk

Book 5: Trouble Brewing

Book 6: Cold Drip

Book 7: Roast Date

Be sure to sign up now for Heather's newsletter at heatherdaygilbert.com for updates, special deals, & giveaways!

And if you enjoyed this book, please be sure to review online and share with your friends about this series!

Thank you!

About the Author:

Heather Day Gilbert has been a "dog person" ever since she was nine years old, when a stray dog named Brownie showed up at her family's doorstep. Growing up, Heather considered Brownie one of her best friends, and, like Macy, she's had a dog in her life ever since. Many of the dog and cat antics in the *Barks & Beans Cafe* series are drawn from real-life experiences (unfortunately, the washing machine flooding incident with Stormy in Book 4 was all-too-real).

This series is based in the real town of Lewisburg, West Virginia, which has been voted "Coolest Small Town in America" by Budget Travel. Heather and her husband regularly visit the quaint town to do on-the-spot research for the Barks & Beans Cafe series.

Heather's also an avid Agatha Christie fan, and would love to someday own all her books. Her favorite Agatha mystery is *Ordeal by Innocence*.

Heather enjoys conversing with her readers via her email newsletter, and she occasionally weaves her readers' dogs into this series as shelter dogs.

Sign up for more dog and book discussions, West Virginia photos, and all the latest on the *Barks & Beans Cafe* series at www.heatherdaygilbert.com!

Printed in Great Britain
by Amazon

28919652R00057